MONKEY
IN SPACE

For Clara, with love

J.L.

ORCHARD BOOKS
96 Leonard Street, London EC2A 4RH
Orchard Books Australia
14 Mars Road, Lane Cove, NSW 2066
Text © Hiawyn Oram 1996
Illustrations © Judith Lawton 1996
First published in Great Britain 1996
First paperback publication 1997
The right of Hiawyn Oram to be identified as the Author
and Judith Lawton as the Illustrator of this Work
has been asserted by them in accordance with the
Copyright, Designs and Patents Act, 1988.
A CIP catalogue record for this book is available
from the British Library.
1 86039 168 0 (hardback)
1 86039 430 2(paperback)
Printed in Great Britain.

MONKEY IN SPACE

The story of Miss Baker

Hiawyn Oram

Illustrated by
Judith Lawton

ORCHARD BOOKS

Read about your favourite animals in
these other Animal Heroes...

Dog in Danger
*The story of Sidney and the
Hedgehogs*

Dolphin SOS!
The story of Nemo and Lemo

Cat in a Corner
The story of Robertson

Chi was a tiny squirrel monkey
who loved showing off.
"Look at me!
Look at me!" she cried
to her friends
as she scampered
through the tree tops.
"Am I fearless?
Am I fast?
Can I fly or can I fly?

Come on! Follow me...!
...If you dare!"
Her friends couldn't resist.
They followed her.

Then one day
they followed her
where even she didn't mean to go.
They followed her into a trap...

...and found themselves
on an aeroplane
on their way
to America!

The other monkeys
rattled at their cages.
"Let us out!"
"We want our jungle!"
"We want Peru!"
Chi watched the clouds float by.
She watched the ground come up

to meet the plane.
She watched
men in white coats
swarm towards them...
and she stayed calm.
"I shall just think of it
as another adventure..."

The men in white coats
took them to a long room
full of cages.
The cages were full of animals.
"Where are we?"
screeched Chi's friends.
"Where are the rivers?"
"Where are the trees?"
"Are there good frogs here?"

"What's going to happen to us?"
A large chimp stuck his nose
through his cage bars.
"I'll tell you what's going
to happen to you...
First you're going to be trained.
And then you're going to be launched!"
Trained and launched!
Chi liked the sound of that.
Especially launched.

It sounded like a great chance
to show off.
"I can't wait to begin!"
she cried.
She didn't have to wait long.
The next day
the men in white
gave her lots of tests
to see if she was fit.

Brilliant!
Chi passed them all
with flying colours!
One of the men
gave her a biscuit.
"Hmm. Not exactly frog,"
said Chi.
"But not bad, Big-eyes.

Now is that it?
Am I trained?
Can I get launched?"

Big-eyes laughed
and stroked her.
"Your training starts tomorrow.
And you're going to do well.
I can feel it.
But I have to warn you.
It's tough."

And it was tough.
Even for a monkey
as cool as Chi.
She didn't mind the hot chamber...
but she hated the cold!
"Hey, Big-eyes, lend me a coat!"

She could just about stand
the deafening noise
and being spun and tumbled
and shaken and rocked...

...but she hated being
without enough air.
"Don't you guys realise
everyone's got to breathe?"
she screeched.

"Whew!"
she cried at Big-eyes
when she got out.
"NOW is that it.
NOW can I get launched?"
Big-eyes gave her a banana.

"You're doing great.
In fact you're doing so well
you've been chosen
for a pretend test flight!
And we've named you Miss Baker
after the famous airwoman!"

With five other monkeys,
the now-Miss-Baker
was put in a new machine.
It wasn't a space rocket
and it wasn't in space.
But it certainly felt like it.
"Is this being launched?"
she asked the monkey beside her.

"Who knows? Who cares?"
he answered.
"All I say is, do it,
get through it.
And by the way,
as we'll be working together,
the name's Able."
"Miss Baker," said Chi.
"After the famous one, you know...
WHOO....OOOPS!"

The noise
and the shaking...

...and the rocking
and the rolling
of take-off began.

Some of the other monkeys
became very upset.
But not Able and Miss Baker.
They stayed cool and calm
through it all.
When it was over,
Big-eyes and the technicians
gave them a round of applause.

"We've still got to get
the go-ahead,"
Big-eyes whispered.
"But when we do,
I'm willing to bet
it's going to be you and Able!"

"Going-to-be-you-and-Able!"
Miss Baker announced
to the dormitory.
"Now that has to mean
launched! Doesn't it?"

"Well, it beats me
why you're so
excited about it,"
said the big chimp.

"Don't you see?
You're being used by these people.
They want to get launched themselves.
Only they're afraid to go first."
"Well I'm not afraid!"
said Miss Baker proudly.

"And I like my work here
and I like working with Big-eyes.
So there!"

"And besides,"
said Able sleepily,
"It may be the only way
out of here."

And the next day
Miss Baker and Able
were taken from
the animal dormitory.

They were given
their own rooms
and special food.
They were checked
and re-checked
and prepared
for a real space flight.

Miss Baker loved
all the attention.
"Though I do wish
you'd get on with it!"
she complained to Big-eyes.
And at last
the big day came.
They were taken to the
Rocket Launching Site
called Cape Canaveral.

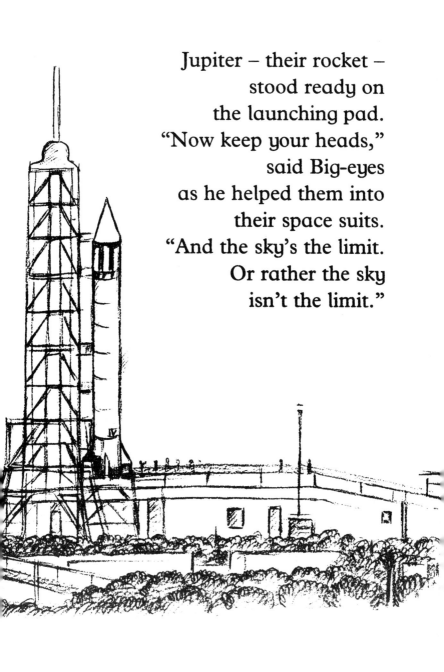

Jupiter – their rocket –
stood ready on
the launching pad.
"Now keep your heads,"
said Big-eyes
as he helped them into
their space suits.
"And the sky's the limit.
Or rather the sky
isn't the limit."

They were strapped
into their seats.
And the countdown began.

There was a roar.
The rocket cone began to shake...
four...three...two...one...zero...
LIFT-OFF!

Miss Baker's training
had prepared her well.
She was startled.
But only for a moment.
When the noise and the shaking
stopped she sat up
as alert as ever.
"Right. Now what?"
"Sit back and enjoy the view,
I suppose," said Able.

"What view?"
said Miss Baker.
"There must be more
to being launched than this.
Where's the adventure?
Where's the excitement?
Where's the chance of showing off?"
Of course she did not know
they were doing something
very exciting.

They were speeding
at great speed in space!
But down on the ground
Big-eyes and the men in white knew.
They also knew they were coming
to the most dangerous part
of the journey –
returning to earth.

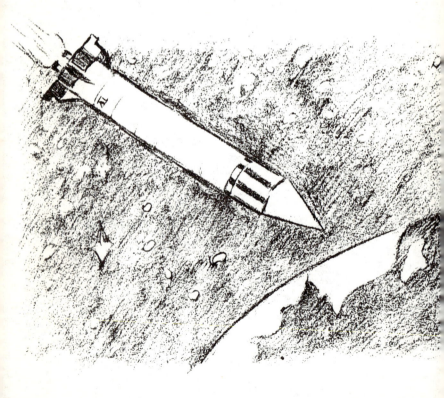

They knew that if anything
went wrong, their rocket
could burst into flames
and burn up.
Big-eyes closed his eyes
and prayed!

The rocket began to shudder
and shake.
Miss Baker and Able
were thrown back
into their seats
with an incredible force.

Then, down on the ground,
the men in white cheered!
It was all over
and everything was fine!
Miss Baker and Able
were bobbing about
in their rocket
in the middle
of the ocean.

"And where's Big-eyes?"
Miss Baker asked
when the recovery team
arrived.
"Because, all I can say is,
if that was being launched
what was all the
song and dance about?

And, by the way,
did he send me
something to eat
'cos I'm famished?"
One of the men
gave her a cracker
and a banana.

He also gave her a cuddle
from Big-eyes.
"He couldn't be here.
But he asked me
to tell you how proud he is.
As we all are.
For you, Miss Baker, ma'am,
are now officially the
first lady in space!"

It didn't mean much
to Miss Baker then,
for she had fallen asleep
in the man's arms.

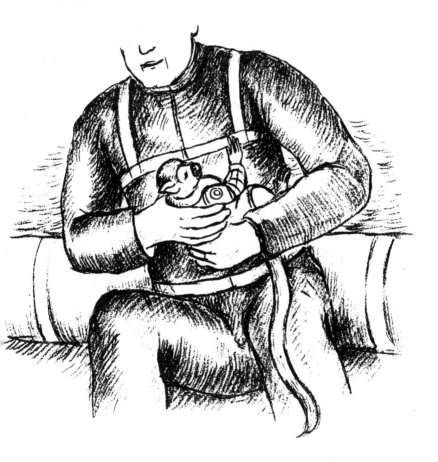

But when she woke up
it certainly did.
She was the toast
of America!
"Now THIS is
more like it!"
she said.
"THIS is what I call
being launched!"
She posed for hundreds
and hundreds
of press pictures
and showed off
to her heart's content.

She was flown around
the country
in her own private plane.
And given the run
of the White House
for a few hours.
She went on television
every day for weeks
and had a lot to say.
"Good morning
America...
good morning..."

"In my early days
in the jungles of Peru
I was always first
flying through the trees,
where no others dared.
So it's been a small leap
to being first
flying through space...

Oh and by the way
say hello to my
good friend Able, here,
who came with me..."

And finally she became
such a favourite
with the American people
that a special home
was built for her
in the Space Centre
in Alabama...
exactly like a jungle!

Her only sadness was
she never saw Able again.
But she found a way
of keeping his memory alive.
"Big George," she announced
to her friend, Big George.
"I have decided to re-name you Able.
After the famous one,
don't you know...
Now...did I ever tell you
the story...."

MONKEY IN SPACE
is based
on the true story
of the first monkeys
known to have survived
flight in space.
The author has changed the
names of any people
and put words into the
mouths of the animals.
It is sad but true that
Miss Baker never saw Able
again because he died
after an operation
soon after their flight.